MR. ADVENTURE

originated by Roger Hargreaves

Written and illustrated by Adam Hargreaves

Grosset & Dunlap
An Imprint of Penguin Random House

Mr. Adventure liked going on vacation, but not the kind of vacation that you and I go on.

He thought beaches were boring.

He wanted the thrill and excitement of an adventure vacation.

He liked to go to places that would make your hair stand on end.

Mr. Adventure went on vacation exploring icy, frozen wastelands.

He went on vacation diving in the deep, blue, bottomless oceans.

He went on vacation canoeing in far-flung,
steamy jungles.

He did not go to the pier to get ice cream.

However, this year, Mr. Adventure had a problem.

He did not have enough money to go on one of his wild adventures.

To go on a new adventure, he would need to get a job.

So that's what he did.

He got a job as a letter carrier.

But being Mr. Adventure, he found delivering letters into mailboxes rather boring.

So, to make it more interesting, he took his mountaineering gear to work with him and climbed the wall of each house and delivered the letters down the chimney.

This certainly made delivering letters more exciting, however, it also made it much slower, and everybody's letters arrived covered in soot.

So he was told not to come back to work at the post office.

The next job he got was as a plumber.

And of course, Mr. Adventure found plumbing boring.

To make it more exciting, Mr. Adventure took his canoe to work when he went to fix a leak.

This did make plumbing more exciting, but it also made people's houses wetter.

Much, much wetter.

And so he was fired from his plumbing job.

And it turned out that wearing skis to his construction job was also not a very good idea.

Things were not going well.

He had not saved a penny.

He looked longingly at the map on his wall.

How he wished he could go on a real adventure.

And then Mr. Adventure got a job as a fireman.

His first job was to climb a very tall tree to save a cat.

This was not boring.

The next day he had to break down a door with an ax.

This was definitely not boring.

12

And the next day he had to put out a fire in a burning house.

Mr. Adventure had found a job that he liked.

A job that suited him down to the ground and right up to the top of the ladder.

In no time at all, Mr. Adventure had saved enough money to go on vacation.

Enough money to go to the wildest, woolliest, most dangerous place you could think of in the whole wide world.

So where did Mr. Adventure go?

Why, he stayed at home!

Being a fireman was a much greater adventure. Although, next year he is planning a trip to . . .

. . . the moon!